T0099843

THE FUTURE OF CONSCIOUSNESS

CLEM STEIN

authorHOUSE®

AuthorHouse™
1663 Liberty Drive
Bloomington, IN 47403
www.authorhouse.com
Phone: 1-800-839-8640

First published by AuthorHouse 9/1/2011

ISBN: 978-1-4567-1434-5 (sc)
ISBN: 978-1-4567-1432-1 (e)

Library of Congress Control Number: 2011908047

Printed in the United States of America

CONTENTS

FOREWORD

BY THE YEAR 2258, RELIGIONS, OR life reward systems (LRS), were totally discredited. All of the myths, miracles, and magic had been disproved. The world's population, with a few exceptions, believed that it was nonsense to say "In God we trust" or "God bless America" in what was left of the United States. Even the immense power block of China and India, the leading world powers, had given up deities.

This is not a normal book foreword; it is a fast forward. We need to fast forward about three hundred years into the future and not look at the past, which of course would be a fast rewind. The signs leading to the assumptions made by this book, when it deals with the future, are everywhere to be seen today. However, the situation is that most people won't or can't see too far beyond the end of their nose. They incorrectly assume that everyone believes what they believe and not too often question the path they take, as most people like the path of least resistance.

It is very uncomfortable to really look at what you are doing. It is disturbing to question commonly held beliefs. If someone called you common, you would be insulted. Almost no one paddles upstream. Almost no one walks up the mountain so that he or she can ski down. People did, of course, walk up mountains carrying their skis and a lunch, before ski lifts were invented. With that invention went a way of life and a style of living. But what really went away, and was much more significant, was a way of thinking.

The international homogenization of the human race is credited with the race's ultimate survival into the future. So insidious and easy is this acceptance that it is not noticed. The incredible lack of a widespread catastrophe or the disastrous predicted human reaction with the inevitable conclusion of the death of God, no life after death, and the realization of a cosmos overflowing with life forms, most of them far superior to earth's, just didn't happen. This realization was greeted with a big "so what." Water did not stop flowing from the pipes in people's shelters. Electricity still came out of the wall receptacles. The homogenized population did what it always did. It picked up the master entertainment controller, a device not unlike a present-day television remote control, and clicked its way somewhere else, while a few nuts, like the present-day's Rush Limbaughs, made complete asses of themselves, believing they were here to save the world as they saw it.

Science had finally provided answers to the age-old questions that had given religions the power and ability to control the world and its people for so long and generate so much misery and at such a cost.

The only real problem, however, was still somewhat the same. Where was the comfort to come from when individuals, no matter how powerful and wealthy, gave up the ghost? By 2300, we are not talking about physical comfort or prolonging physical life. That had all been taken care of. The average life span of individuals in developed societies was somewhere between 200 and 250 years. A long life, body replacement parts, and an almost pain-free existence were taken for granted. Some very wealthy individuals, in hopes of some self-awareness and consciousness breakthrough, hung around for even longer at a risk of some pain and a bit of peer disgust.

While everyone now knew there was no God, no hell or heaven, and no life after death, they still had a very difficult time coming to grips with the central issues so dominated in innuendos by all religions in the past. The central issues still were focused upon self-worth, self-consciousness, and the fear of a loss of self-awareness.

People still didn't want to just "blink out" and forget themselves or be forgotten by others. Now that everyone lived two hundred years or more, they eventually realized they just wanted to put down their worn-out body and avoid all the physical assaults. Nirvana was close to the idea, but alas, no cigar. However, with the advances of manufactured intelligence and self-awareness (I hate the term "artificial intelligence"), real hope was springing up.

So let's fast forward to 2312+, the passing-on palaces, and see what our scientific friend Hal was putting together.

THE FUTURE OF CONSCIOUSNESS

IN THE BEGINNING

HAL MUSED THAT IF YOU JUST looked, you certainly could see the end of lifestyle reward systems (LRS) coming. It was all so obvious that a glance would have sufficed. You really didn't have to look very far. A good example was in Europe, specifically France. There, the Church had simply given their buildings to the government because the cost of the upkeep was beyond their ability to maintain. Over a thousand years after laying the cornerstone of Notre Dame in Paris, the last pope cleaned out the treasury, sold as many assets as he could, did a fraudulent initial public offering (IPO) using the remaining real estate, left for somewhere, and couldn't be found at the time of this writing. The buildings were falling apart and empty anyway. Very few people were showing up, and those who did came there to wonder at the lack of intellect and the gullibility of the people who, in the past, believed the unsupportable teachings hallowed in those halls.

This was also true for any lifestyle reward system that was over a thousand years old. After studying these systems and the current behavior of the world's population, Hal determined that with the exception of a few illiterates in back-road cloisters and high-mountain Himalayan enclaves, people had finally come to grips with the fact that they weren't afraid of dying. They understood now that there was not a soul, a hell, or a heaven, but just a loss of self-consciousness. This intellectual realization, however, did not take away the longing to be immortal, which, of course, religions, philosophies, and LRS had catered to since almost the dawn of time.

Hal thought that perhaps this transition of beliefs had begun back in the early 2000s, when science had figured out how to replicate and produce basic DNA, the building block of all life. Scientists figured out how to do this in much the same way that nature had by constructing the double helix from the chemical soup that had been deposited on the earth 3 billion years earlier from serendipitous collisions with planetoids and meteors that had started life off after a big bang.

All of the prior lifestyle value and reward systems, codes of conduct, and world rules that were based on ascended men, virginal women, holy cows, wise men, sitting fat statues. examples, self-examination, red robes, seventy-two virgins if you were good, mechanical prayer wheels, planet worship, and solar-centered beliefs, had finally been proven to have no real basis. In fact, it was widely accepted that all of those philosophies, as practiced by their ardent followers, and their insistence on their beliefs being the only right ones, had created most of the problems that kept people killing each other for man's entire history.

What it had all boiled down to was the control of real estate and the world's wealth by the few, for the desecration of the many. How mankind could have been so ignorant and blind for so long now seemed to be incomprehensible even to the masses.

INEVITABILITY

HAL HAD TAKEN A LOT OF undergraduate science history and religious history courses. He had really tried to wrap himself around the pretext of most of the LRS. He had taken time off from "hard" science to gain a deeper insight into what he feared was adding ammunition to armory that would further destroy faith—in anything. However, with the passing of the popularity of the lifestyle reward systems (better known as religions) as the opiate of the masses, a substitute system and then an industry grew up to deal with the inevitability of every man.

The gap—created by the lack of a promised land, rewards for living a "good life" (or a life after death)—had to be filled! People realized that all that had come before was nonsense;

however, it was nonsense that allowed them to avoid thinking about the fact that someday, in the not-too-distant future, they would no longer have self-awareness and be conscious. They would no longer exist.

The realization that they would no longer exist drove some humans to the brink of sanity and some over the brink. It simply was unthinkable that after thousands of years of being told that it was going to be okay—that if you were a nice, kind person and followed any religion's template for the rules of living your life you would have some kind of reward and existence after your body gave up and died.

When life was hard, when existence was chancy, when microbes and bacteria could end it all in the blink of an eye, the believed comfort supposedly generated by LRS made some kind of sense. Now, in 2312, man had progressed to a life span of 250 years and more. Food, energy, and comfort were universally available. LRS just weren't needed anymore.

But something was needed to fill the comfort void, the black hole in the psyche of man. Lots of things had been tried, but they all seemed to just put Band-Aids on the problem. It was still difficult to get people to face the inevitable. So how do you eliminate ignorance? Right, with education.

A new movement started to help man deal with the inevitable fact that he was going to die. If you think about it, it is hilarious that when death takes a family member, there is calamity and people are stunned. Some people are even incredulous at the obvious. Death is even looked on as a catastrophe. People display their despair, and wailing and crying take over what was left of reason and sanity. The only important and undeniable inevitability is man's death, and yet he had no philosophy for this inevitability. Religions and cults denied death by offering hope of life after death and packaged this message in organized movements. However, if you remove the fear of death and the fear generated by guilt in LRS, you will still have the fact that death is inevitable.

What was becoming apparent and brought some peace of mind was the extension of longevity. What came with long life was a surprising realization that had been known but ignored for centuries, and it was this: Most people just get tired of living. At an informal dinner one evening at the Montana Scientific Mountain office, Hal got into a discussion that led to a group conclusion that many thoughtful people, after living for 250 or more years, just want to quit. They had "been there and done that," seen that before, and didn't want to change anymore. They were sick and tired of the same old thing, and even the intellectually unique and gifted just said "enough."

This realization was rapturous. It did not involve faith. It was much deeper than that. It was profound. This realization compensated for a life of sadness and struggle that only had a glimpse of ecstasy.

A STUMBLING STEP

"SAM, DO YOU REMEMBER CARL SAGAN?"

"Who?"

Hal repeated, "Carl Sagan! You know, he hosted a science TV show on NPR that explored the galaxy way back in the late 1900s."

"Oh yeah, don't we have copies of his program in the science history files?"

Hal thought for a moment and said, "Oh, I'm sure they are there somewhere."

Sagan had taken an interesting interim step. Back in the twentieth century he was so bright and outside the box that he ended up on national public television. The program he hosted earned fantastic ratings because it explored the galaxy.

Well, kind of. It was televised from a spaceship stage set. All the Trekkies and science fiction fans could gather around their TV sets and watch as this brilliant man, who looked just like you and me, talked about the universe in everyday terms and words.

Then something happened to Dr. Carl Sagan, something that took the wind out of his sails and put his star drive in neutral. All of a sudden it made this man look at what he was doing. He was diagnosed with terminal cancer. He went from being a young, brilliant, wealthy, good-looking television celebrity to someone who had, at the most, two years to live. In the twentieth century, you were only as good as your last show, and if you created a problem, you were finished.

Dr. Sagan, one of the great communicating minds of the twentieth century, tried to come to grips with the fact that in about 1,036,800 minutes, 17,280 hours, 720 days, or 24 months, he would no longer exist. So to keep his sanity, and to bring him some piece of mind, he started a quest to prove that there was a God and life after death. Because of who he was and where he was, he was able to apply to this search all of the scientific tools of the time.

There could be no questioning his motivation, his scientific dedication, and his one-mindedness. He was going to be gone in twenty-four months. He really wanted to know where he was going to end up and what was ahead. He used every avenue and tool that his elevated position gave him. He worked 24-7 for two years until he dropped dead at age sixty-two.

One of his final statements was: "After everything I have done, after all of my research, after my complete focus on this task, I can find no scientific evidence of life after death, or a god." Then he died. That may have been the start of the end of the relevance of LRS. That utterance, however, still left the problem that everyone has to face. It was not the last word on the subject by any chance, and it really did kick off a movement that was covertly financed and encouraged by most of the major lifestyle reward system's organizations, the religions of the world. At first Hal was very unhappy with Sagan's conclusion, but he just couldn't seem to argue with it. However, it was being tossed around that everyone had a "personal God" in those days and maybe Sagan just couldn't locate his! People who followed this story in the twentieth century all mostly looked for other reasons to ignore his findings or just flipped off the TV.

The basic premise of that movement was kind of a throwback to the idea of ultimate control and a complete lack of—you should pardon the pun—"faith" in man. Man was no good at all and was basically a raging monster held in control by the fear of ultimate punishment and a "hell" for the bad guys and a "heaven" for the good guys.

In reaction, religious people wrote books and made films, some of which were semi-documentaries that explored the concept of a dead God. Many religions, hysterically, felt that if God was dead, it would be the end of the world. They proclaimed that all societies—whether they worshipped cows, profits, or statues, or they gave some credence to a life after death—would simply fall apart. They said that, in ninety days, law and order would break down, there would be a loss of the worldwide power grid, and then water would stop flowing from the pipes in your home. Believe it or not, people wrote serious books on this subject, which were published and made the best-seller lists. One of the more entertaining efforts was by Ron Currie, Jr., titled so originally *God Is Dead*. One of the funnier parts of this book is a chapter about God as a dog where the author attributes some feeling of guilt to LRS for having "taken the world population's meager belongings in exchange for lies, however well-intentioned those lies were."

What religions wouldn't face was the fact that they were simply transient. Organized religions were forgetting that they had only been around for a few thousand years—a blink of the eternal eye, so to speak—and while men in the beginning used to knock each other over the heads and take what they wanted, they soon learned that the guy with the biggest club didn't always get what he was after. The slow process of learning to get along so that you could get what you wanted became apparent to the survivors.

Cataclysmic action movies had no effect on the population except to set new box office records and produce terrible sequels to the original movies as the directors tried to top each other with stunts and computer-generated special effects. It was becoming obvious that the fear of death still existed, but that was really as far as it went. It was just like so many other situations. People knew that if they became fat and ruined their lungs by smoking, they were dead. They knew that but couldn't, wouldn't, or didn't want to change. Okay, so God was dead. They would deal with that later.

Religious people attempted to raise these thoughts in the consciousness of the masses. The messages were subtle and spongy and didn't deal with a dead God but just an end to the world. Films, like *On the Beach* with Fred Astaire, from the 1960s dealt with it by putting the end of the world in the hands of man because of the fallout from a nuclear war. The film ends with the cessation of all human life but leaves a warning by saying that there was still time.

We all now know that there is no way to prove or disprove that there ever has been spiritual or mystical life after death. At least there hasn't been life like we would want it to be. All it has ever been is an argument about semantics and definitions.

Another great mind of the twentieth century almost sparked a trend. When Albert Einstein died in 1955, within seven hours of his death, his brain had been removed and preserved for study. Whether his brain was removed with his permission is still a matter of conjecture. In any case, this man was one of the foremost geniuses of the twentieth century. You know E = mc2.

Einstein's brain was removed and chopped up into pieces, sliced like a good Italian air-dried ham, and studied by anyone who could get their hands on a slice. Before it was chopped up into pieces, it was photographed and measured, and it was found to have smaller regions than most other people in the area of the brain that took care of speech and language skills, but it had larger areas that dealt with spatial and numerical issues. How much of a surprise was that?

The fellow who was doing the research was relieved from his medical position at Princeton. In 1980, Berkeley Professor Marian Diamond got Tom Harvey, the keeper of Einstein's grey matter, to give her samples of Einstein's brain. She discovered that Einstein's brain had more glial cells per neurons than most other brains she had studied. Glial cells provide support and nutrition in the brain from myelin and participate in signal transmission. That was a very important bit of information for Hal as he considered how he would keep the new big brain (BB) alive and well and what to look for in approaching signal transmission.

THE POWER OF ELECTRICITY

IT WAS PROVEN A LONG TIME ago in the 1960s that a small electrical charge or electrical field leaves your body when you die. But it is just a moment, and, at least until now, it has not been digitally readable.

Some religious cults preached that your personal codes were digitalized within this field as it left your body and the world forever, and it also contained your consciousness. This charge went out of you to join with a massive spiritual and universal consciousness that would recycle you. This was how you would live again. You would be reincarnated. Some cults believed and taught that there was a slight possibility that you may have some recollection of your prior existence. This was all very powerful stuff, and some very far-thinking socially aware business opportunists came up with a terrific money-making plan.

And that was how and why they built the "passing-on palaces" where, if you had enough money, you went to die. It was an exclusive club. It was based not just on your wealth, but supposedly there were other criteria.

But let's be frank. Money seems to get you a place in line. The perceptive technology to detect, grasp, and record your essence as it left your body in the form of a minute electrical charge grew out of a lot of space science and medical research. It was all integrated, adapted, and wired together by some very bright science and business types, like Steve Jobs of Apple, a pioneering computer company in the twentieth century.

These people, for the most part, believed in what they were doing. When they passed on, they had their electric body charge recorded, just in case it was going to work. By the way, getting your electrical charge digitalized was one of the benefits given to employees of the company, along with the use of the company health spa and lunchroom.

When you died in a "palace," they used their technical know-how and trapped your minute electrical field as it left your body. The electrical field would be digitalized and encoded on a silicon chip. The plan was that your chip would then be stored—for a fee, of course—until sometime in the future when the priests of their cult, perhaps, would figure out how to read the chip and bring back your memories and consciousness. You would be living again, or at least your consciousness would be. (Make sure you read all the fine print on the disclosures of the passing-on palace's contract.) Like all other contracts and fine print, nothing was guaranteed except that they would cash your check and do the best they could to increase your net worth, which you had to deed to them as part of the contract to safeguard your chip.

This idea had so much appeal that passing-on palaces grew to be a major franchise business. They were like the KFC of the live-forever cults. (KFC in this case means "keep forever consciousness," not to be confused with Kentucky Fried Chicken, although by the year 2235 the palaces had "stores" on what seemed like every other corner.)

Of course, this turned out to be a rework of the half-brained idea of cryonics. The idea there was that if your old, sick body was frozen when you died, someone would be able to thaw you out sometime in the future and repair you. After you were defrosted, you would be fixed up and able to live again. Some people were so panicked at the thought of not being anymore that they went a step further. They were frozen before their death, figuring some kind of life force might remain in their frozen body and they would have a better chance of reincarnation than those folks who waited until they were dead to be frozen. I think a baseball player or two did this, but it was feared that the steroids they had used in life to bulk up for their performance duties may have created a problem while they are being thawed. Being that aggressive, however, put them in the minority.

It was a perfect example of the state of panic of wealthy people who could afford to cover that base just in case there may be some truth to the process—which, of course, there wasn't.

I'D LIKE TWO OF ME, PLEASE

ANOTHER THEORY THAT WAS INDEED PRACTICED, but not very well known, was the insidious offshoot from cryonics: immortality by cloning. The very wealthy found the profit-centered medical doctors of the world and funded their "research" into cloning.

If you had enough money, you could get cloned, and then clone husbandry was practiced until the clone reached puberty. At that time, the clone was terminated and its parts harvested. These parts were hermetically sealed in packages and were flash-frozen using the learned skills from failed cryogenics science. By that time, cryogenic scientists were out of a job and looking for work, and so it was a match made in a paranoid heaven.

There were also manufacturing benefits and a potential for some profits as an offshoot of this practice. While frozen food had been around for hundreds of years, no one seemed to want to have cloned body parts next to the rib roast or pigs' feet in their freezer. Hal understood that if you went through all the trouble and expense of cloning yourself, there had to be a better place than your kitchen freezer to keep your bid for immortality safe. So, to help in the funding of his scientific research and the Montana Mountain Scientific Corporation, on the New York Stock Exchange as MMSC, Hal developed a super-efficient "clone keeper." It was about the size of a Coleman cooler. It was a real mechanical marvel. Totally self-powered and self-contained, it was completely independent of any outside power source. After your clone was terminated and the parts harvested, a service business packed your parts and stored them away in this cooler—which would be very subzero, almost to absolute zero—and then the cooler was delivered any place you specified. The system was guaranteed to perform for a hundred years, which seemed to satisfy most of the customers.

This idea was legal at the time, because euthanasia laws were universal and the clone was considered the personal property of the person from whom it was created. The results were obvious. If you could afford to do this, you had a freezer full of spare parts.

Advanced stem cell research also started to play a part in all of this, as you could now scrape the inside of your cheek, and the clinics you endowed through your generosity would grow the parts you needed or wanted. However, all of these processes required cutting and pasting, and even with the advances in surgery, it still meant going under a knife, and some people just didn't like that.

HERE'S WOOFIE!

A REALLY INTERESTING ASIDE TOOK PLACE in the first decade of the twenty-first century. People had become absolutely crazy about animals. From pets, to animals in the wild, to farm animals, there was some kind of a group that had one objection or another to, or plans for, the protection of animals that were now endowed with all kinds of human characteristics. One of the groups was just too interesting to let its story go untold.

People for the Ethical Treatment of Animals (PETA) offered a million-dollar prize to the first developer of laboratory meat. This "bone fide" offer really excited the International In Vitro Meat Symposium to the point that the lab meat movement really got under way.

This movement, however, seemed to insult or infuriate everyone but the owners of the worldwide McDonald's restaurant chain who found a way to underwrite it with all kinds of cash. This franchise hamburger company, desperate to remain on every other corner around the world, could see the future of chicken nuggets' profits, based on not having to grow chickens from eggs, feed and house chicks, kill them, remove the flesh from their bones, form them into nuggets, bread them with a coating, and then deep-fry them. Yummy! Please don't forget dipping sauces.

With chicken flesh, both dark and white meat, grown from a stem cell started in a nutritive solution in a laboratory, you could eliminate all the messy steps in the process from embryo to nugget. It should make the animal people happy, and profits would soar. However, the farmers didn't care for this idea because they could see where it would lead.

The movement had to be sold to the public. By this time, if you asked children where milk came from, most kids didn't have the vaguest idea, or they would say it came from the supermarket. It was difficult to explain to them that they were drinking a liquid produced from grass that was eaten by a large grazing animal with four stomachs, that the liquid was then squeezed from the animal breast, and this animal was forced to continually produce more milk by taking it from her twice every day. The really cruel thing was that the milk was intended for the animal's offspring, which it was designed to nourish, and of course the offspring was denied the liquid so that the kids could have it. The dairy associations across the country, however, never mentioned this sequence of events to get the milk to the kid's table.

In a survey conducted by an animal rights survey group, when children were told this story they either didn't understand or, if they did, they had one of two reactions. They either got sick to their stomachs and ran from the room or said, "Gosh, that's kind of weird, but I'm not going to cry over spilled milk."

This entire movement to build meat in a lab was an offshoot from the medical research of stem cell replacement parts for humans. Some very bright marketing people, in conjunction with food scientists and folks who wanted to solve the problem that a third of the world's people were going to bed hungry every night, got together and came up with in vitro meat production.

In the beginning, they felt that to produce chicken flesh from chicken stem cells in a lab was perhaps the answer to the world's hunger problem. Then, of course, the idea grew—you should pardon the pun—to producing pork from pig stem cells and beef from cattle stem cells, all nice and neat in a laboratory without breeding, birthing, feeding, housing, killing, butchering, and all the messy problems, like methane production in the atmosphere and everything else related to animal husbandry.

Just a small aside here. In the first half of the twenty-first century, there were feedlots where cows were kept for a few weeks or a month and fed a special diet so that when they were slaughtered, the flesh had acquired the right amount of fat and corn-fed taste that people liked. Because these feedlots were large—some as large as four hundred acres with thousands of cows, all in one place—the methane produced by these animals made driving by a feedlot a memorable and unpleasant olfactory experience.

I mean, if it walks like a duck, quacks like a duck, it's a duck. Right? But if it tastes like a duck and comes from a duck but doesn't walk or quack like a duck, is it a duck?

Back to our main point. Even with these advances, to Hal it was obvious that the problem was still being approached from the wrong angle.

I AIN'T GOT NO BODY

HAL AND HIS GROUP OF SCIENTISTS at the MMSC concluded that the human body—no matter what you did, how many parts you replaced, and how many times you replaced them—just couldn't survive indefinitely. There comes a point where you just can't patch it any longer, and as the Borg said, continuing this exercise was "futile." Anyway, it wasn't the body that people wanted preserved. It was the consciousness, the feelings, the memories, the experiences, and most of all, the self-awareness. All of these things had nothing to do with the body. We are talking about the brain.

The loss of consciousness or self-awareness always had been the real fear that drove the irrational, unsupportable, and loony religions and do-good movements. Their core appeal was that these groups or their founders knew better than you did, and on top of that, they had the answer in their philosophies.

The people in power always claimed that they had the answers to your ultimate survival, so they took control and ran the world. Con men of this stripe have done more harm in the world and killed more people in the name of peace and God, and in the process they became richer than anyone else.

It is incredible when you look back on what these people have fabricated and distorted to promote and control this fear. If a "good" man was dying, he hopefully felt prepared and, if rich enough or noble, he was surrounded by men in robes holding small smoking fires in pots and chanting words from a dead language.

However, when he breathed his last breath, his offspring and everyone within the man's former sphere of influence said, "Katy, bar the door," and that was the end of his consciousness. The body went into the ground, and the fight was on for everything he had owned before his body got cold.

Here is an almost universally accepted description of what it was like being dead. It seemed overly simple and incomplete, but its beauty lay in the fact that it was simple, didn't take any effort, involved no fear (just some sadness), and got you off the hook for the way you had lived your life. Here is what they believed: When you are dead, it is like when you go to sleep, but you don't dream and you don't wake up. Again, you go to

THE FUTURE OF CONSCIOUSNESS

sleep, you don't dream, and you don't wake up. The beauty, of course, is that you don't know it. If you are ready for that, it is a perfect answer.

Compare that to the other older philosophy's answers, which stated that when you die you come back to earth reincarnated at some level on the food chain, maybe as a worm, and relive your life till you get it right as a worm. Then you get to move up one step at a time on the food chain until you get it right. What is right has always been a bit foggy. Or perhaps you go someplace and are rewarded with seventy-two virgins. (That's heaven, not hell?) It doesn't say what the virgins get or what happens to women who seem to be second-class.

How about this one? You die, go up into the sky, are issued a white robe, are reunited with a bunch of people you never really liked (at least when they came over on weekends), sit on clouds, sing hymns, and tell someone with an insatiable ego sitting on a throne that he or/she is wonderful and so are his or her dad and the ghost sitting on the other side of the throne, and you get to do this for eternity. For space travel fans, you achieve perfect unity with the universe; however, that may not take into consideration the big bang theory.

LIFESTYLE REWARD SYSTEMS

IF YOU EXAMINE THE LIFESTYLE REWARD systems in the last chapter, the most obvious question that comes up is how on earth people in power ever got anyone to believe them. The Christian story, while adapting ideas from earlier myths so as to include as many people as possible, was interesting.

It said that a Jewish boy was born to a lady who had never had sex but was engaged in a relationship at the time. The boy became a carpenter and practiced his trade for about thirty years. He then got tired of pounding nails and decided that he was the son of the Jewish God and was sent to save mankind from hell. The Jews in charge of the temple at that time didn't buy it. Anyway, he put down the tools of the trade and started telling people who he was. He picked up a group of fishermen whose boats he may have repaired when he was a carpenter.

This turned out to be a good idea, as the ex-fisherman sometimes furnished fish for the crowd if they got hungry. This unlikely group then began a cross-country crusade, or tent show, but without the tent. They did this for about three years, covering a geographic area about the size of the greater Los Angeles basin. They held mass group meetings, passed the plate, and did well. Then they came to the attention of the Jewish and Roman officials.

The Jews were able to convince the Roman government that, while the guy was just some nut, he was, after all, preaching revolution, so they got him arrested. The arrest was prompted by the carpenter going into the Jewish temple and upsetting the tables from which the Jews were selling trinkets and religious objects.

A Roman official, who apparently did a lot of flying and was nicknamed Pilot, had him arrested, put him on trial, and got him convicted of plotting against Rome. Pilot was a smart politician, and so to cover his ass and keep his hands clean, he put the convicted carpenter in front of a Jewish stacked crowd and said, "You make the choice." As part of a celebration of some Roman holiday he asked the crowd, "Should I let the carpenter go free or free this other convicted crook?"

The crowd picked the other guy. Pilot then asked one of his slaves to bring him a bowl of water and a towel and in front of the crowd washed his hands, dried them, and said, "I wash my hands of all of this. It is your decision, not mine." And so, to no one's surprise, they executed the carpenter. It was kind of like the first century's "where is the beef" political statements. You know the kind of statements that live in infamy.

Now, eleven of the twelve men who were the carpenter's followers had a problem. They had sold their fishing boats, and they liked their new lifestyle. There are, and always have been, many theories about what really happened, but generally it goes like this: Someone removed the carpenter's body from a tomb that had been lent to them after his execution, and they got rid of the body. The twelfth follower didn't stick around, as he had been paid in silver coins by the Romans or Jews—we don't know who—to point out, or finger, the carpenter, who was hanging out in a garden where he was arrested.

The eleven remaining guys all agreed that they would stick to the story that the carpenter had risen from the dead after three days in the tomb, talked with them, and then ascended out of sight on a cloud into the sky. They all stuck to the story, and some of them got killed for sticking to it.

One of the twelve, Peter the rock, said that the carpenter had given him the keys to heaven and became the first pope of the Roman Church. He traveled a lot, raised money, and thus began a legacy of two thousand plus years raising money, controlling real estate, and telling people how to live and what would happen to them when they died if they didn't follow the rules.

IT'S FOR YOUR OWN GOOD

ENFORCING THE RULES, HOWEVER, TURNED OUT to be no easy task. To accomplish this the Church used about every device they could think of, because if you didn't say you believed their story and contribute to the organization's treasury, they may ask you to reconsider, and to consider the consequences if you didn't play along.

Can you imagine running one of the world's largest organizations, not paying taxes on your real estate or paying your managers, and insisting your story was true? This kind of reminded Hal of Adolf Hitler. You may remember reading about World War II. Hitler said the bigger the lie and the more you repeat it and the more outrageous it is, the easier it is to get it accepted and believed.

To back up Hitler's belief in screaming lies, a Stanford University study in the early 2000s said that students—and the ones at Stanford were supposed to be the best and brightest in the nation at the time—when repeatedly exposed (five times) to unsubstantiated claims taken from a website that claimed Coca-Cola (a popular, worthless soft drink) was an effective paint remover were nearly one-third more likely than those who read it only twice to attribute it to *Consumer Reports*, a national magazine about consumer products. (Their second choice was the *National Enquirer*, a scandal sheet, giving it a gloss of credibility.)

Psychologists have suggested that legends (insert your own belief here) propagate by striking an emotional chord you remember, thus religion's appeal. Ideas can be spread by emotional selection rather than by the factual merits. (All the major religions lack hard facts, but have only unsupportable emotional claims.) Encouraging the persistence of falsehoods about any subject by any organized group that wishes to promote its ideas for whatever reasons is done this way. Paraphrasing what the famous Mayor Daley of Chicago said in the mid-1960s, vote early and vote often, lie early and repeat it often.

Here is just a partial list of threats that were used to convince people to accept the story or at least go along with it. They included physical pain, beheading, crucifixion, skinning alive, wars, crusades, burning at the stake, tearing out your beating heart, tossing your body down a stairway, removing limbs and other parts, stretching the body (on the rack), starvation, stoning, sacking, drowning, dunking, damning, and decapitating.

Faced with these alternatives, about a third of the world population (this was before China numbered a billion people) just said oh well, what the hell, and went along with it. The other two-thirds of the world followed some other cockamamie stories that I am not going to take the time to dismantle. Just let it be said they made as little sense and logic as the Roman story, but they did fill the same need: relieving people's fear of death. And they gave the masses some rules to live by, and they gave the leaders the needed power to control people and wealth.

None of these philosophies addressed the real problem. Until manufactured intelligence (MI) came along and memory could be encoded on silicon, the problem could be avoided.

But not any longer.

PROGRESS IS OUR MOST IMPORTANT PRODUCT

ONE NIGHT AFTER AN EXCEPTIONALLY PRODUCTIVE day, Hal and Sam in Hal's private office were sharing a bottle of wine and got to talking about what people now knew they wanted. Sam thought that people just wanted to maintain their self-awareness and consciousness. Hal argued that with the average life span somewhere between 170 to 200 years, and a few diehards living for 285 years, people realized there had to be more to living than just living. Both men who had spent years with numbers and research, they loved the story about an old person who had spent his time calculating what he had put into his body and what his body had put out. He figured out that he had processed enough food and liquid over his life thus far to piss enough to fill an average-sized private swimming pool (a width of 16 feet multiplied by a length of 32 feet multiplied by an average depth of 5.75 feet or 22,360 gallons plus or minus 7 percent). If the excrement he had extruded was laid end to end, it would stretch (his words, not mine) 29.73 miles, plus or minus 8 percent. It was no wonder he had undergone three stem cell bladder replacements and—how shall we put it—four new stem cell-generated assholes.

In the last decade of the twentieth century, things got going with medical professionals regarding understanding and controlling brain waves. In 1999, they unlocked brain patterns for dealing with the alphabet and were making interesting strides in reading and generating brain patterns to control devices. Speech recognition technology had come along in the late 1900s and was applied to controlling machines and computers. Brain wave and conscious pattern control devices were next on the horizon.

The field of cybernetics grew in leaps and bounds. Most things used to be driven solely by economics, the medical profession included. So it focused its research on producing results that would allow paraplegics with artificial limbs to get around like everyone else. This, of course, became passé when developments in stem cell limb-regenerating science advanced to the point where, like a lizard that just grows a new tail when it loses the current one, science could regenerate the body's limbs and parts from the injured person's stem cells.

Using a person's own stem cells solved the problem of rejection of artificial, scavenged, and stolen body parts, which had always triggered the body's immune system. Now that didn't make a difference any longer. It was really a big business for a while.

The knowledge that you could get a new body part if you lost one gave a completely different meaning to contact sporting events and mass entertainment. Imagine what it did for the bull in bull fighting. If people had thought that the fighting between the Romans and gladiators was grisly, they should have been spectators at the new NFL contests and machete-carrying Rollerblade contests that sold out large arenas on a regular basis. While it certainly was uncomfortable to lose some attached part, the fear of risking all to win the player-of-the-year award made sense to some professional athletes.

Whatever was being done back then faced enormous obstacles in the form of political pressure, as a large segment of the world's population, religious fundamentalists, had organized objections to anything that challenged the belief that the world was put together in seven days and the body was the vessel that contained the soul and anything artificial was satanic, evil, ungodly, and to be stamped out.

Along with all this were, of course, gigantic strides in silicon-based devices that could do almost anything. Silicon-based technology typically doubled its processing capacity every two years, but it had been doing this for so many years that it was running into a wall where that just couldn't happen any longer.

Something new, or something that had been discarded

along the way, would have to be found, as silicon's doubling capacity had been reached and it seemed most physical problems had been solved. Most people now understood that self-awareness and continued consciousness still were a mystery.

WHERE DO ANSWERS COME FROM?

IF HAL HAD TRIED TO PREDICT who would come along and solve this problem, there is no way he would have come up with this kind of answer. The ingredients that make up a person who could save the world—the new messiah, the guru of the masses, the born-again leader, or the leader of the intellectual army—would not make up this guy.

Hal thought it was such a waste that the life experiences of the billions of people who had come before were forever lost. When the lights went out behind their eyes and they died, their entire files of lessons, experiences, education, fantasies, dreams, desires, fuckups, hopes, and fears, and the total elements of their very existence were gone. They rotted away with the corpse. They were, of course, unrecoverable.

Sure, there were books, audio and video files, microfilm, and computer banks filled with information. But all of that missed the point. It was not filled with self-awareness and consciousness. These two elements of life, the most important part of life, were missing, gone, erased, terminated.

What was required was the realization that what people really wanted after life was freed consciousness (FC) with participation and responsibility.

Hal knew that after treading the boards for two hundred plus years, even the best of us just wanted to put down the body, not be troubled with the daily crap, and have the good stuff that we had filtered through and distilled in our minds live on. This was so that we felt we had walked this way for some kind of reason and were still valuable and would not be forgotten. It has always been so. Robber barons of the past built libraries and put their names on them to prove to the next generation that they were good guys and had used their wealth to help mankind.

What mankind really wanted in the depths of their minds was to participate in an accessible, responsive, two-way, infinite, eternal source of universal self-conscious awareness that was based upon the collective minds of everyone who wanted to participate and who had gone before. Men wanted to put down the burden of the body and live without using resources, with the exception of a little electricity, and further themselves and future generations.

It wasn't a think tank of PhDs that came upon the idea, but

they were all working on the problem and had been since the demise of all religions. The physicists knew that somewhere in the depths of the big bang theory or some mutation in the evolution of E = mc2 lay the creation answer, but it still eluded them.

Medical professionals had finally tossed in the towel. They just sat back on their laurels and said surgery, cloning, stem cell parts building, and the general practice of good nutrition had been their contribution to mankind, and they should be first in line for any new advancement from any field as their reward for serving mankind since Hippocrates.

Dr. Hal Dabble, PhD, had gone to the University of Wisconsin and had gotten an advanced degree in chemical engineering and a few other advanced degrees. Along the way, he had studied physics, almost dropped engineering to study medicine, and almost became a biologist. Hal was concerned with a lot of things, but in his own way, and not a way that fit perfectly into the rigors of advanced studies. So he had a lot of time to think his own way.

He always said it was not what you thought but how you thought. One of Hal's biggest strengths was his ability to focus. Some people confused this ability and thought him narrow. His response was that a laser is useful because it is focused, and a narrow beam seemed to get things done the way Hal liked.

For some reason, the approach to brain study always seemed to focus on the electrical components and operation of the system. Of course, the biological components of the brain were dissected, and so much research had been done here that the scientists who had been doing it felt the field and they were exhausted.

Back in the early 2000s, much was being made of binaural beats, harmonically layered frequencies, EEG and brain wave images, and stimulated neural development. This was all about the "brave new world" stuff without using chemicals to get you there.

Taking binaural beats in binaural audio a step further and using harmonically layered frequency technology, the brain could be convinced you were having a good time and feeling just great without chemicals. This, of course, at first raised hell with the drug community—no, not Whitehall-Robins Inc., Pfizer, or Bayer, but the underground operators in Mexico, Chile, and Nicaragua.

It was claimed that the use of this process would encourage the formation of new pathways in your brain. Also, its use would increase or expand the production of your neural pathways and produce smoother communication in your brain. However, the part that Hal was interested in had to do with the energy and electrical patterns exercised by this, and that exercise increased the processing power in your brain. This had a lot to do with your brain wave state, and Hal felt that had a connection to your consciousness and your self-awareness.

Not much research had been done on what impact, if

anything, changing frequencies had on the chemicals that were the message carriers between the synapses in the brain, and that was disturbing.

I suppose that I should give you an example of what they were talking about, so here goes: If you feed an audio signal of, say, 110 Hz into your brain via your left ear, and a 120 Hz signal into your right ear, these two signals will mesh in and out of phase, and the brain will then create its own third, or phantom, signal or binaural beat. That signal will be equal to the difference between the two frequencies—in this case, a 10 Hz binaural beat, an entirely new sound.

It was said that the introduction of a binaural beat would cause the brain to resonate in tune to the frequency of that beat. Say you listen to a binaural beat pulsing at 10 Hz, an alpha frequency. That will then trigger your brain to resonate at 10 Hz, which will induce brain waves in the alpha range. This in turn will allow you to induce effortlessly any brain wave state you desire. Now aren't you glad we talked about that?

In the pursuit of his goals, Hal became very concerned about consciousness, self-awareness, and self-consciousness, the very same things people in the twenty-first century were paranoid about. If he could codify consciousness, and have a collective consciousness, how could the information be secured?

Another interesting question Hal was dealing with was whether a state of consciousness could be collected from a living person and, if so, how and where it could be stored and used. The other big question was if the consciousness state could be captured, what would be left in the brain?

SPAM?

FORTUNATELY, THE DEVELOPMENT OF QUANTUM MECHANICS
had—if you will pardon the pun—opened up the field of security. Quantum key distribution allowed for absolutely secure encryption of information exchanges by encoding information keys on single photons.

Hal's MMSC was working on moving single photons around in the brain, based on the theory that, with success, teleportation of quantized states would be a possibility. These photons are so sensitive that there is physically no way to undetectably tamper with them as they travel from sender to receiver. The teleportation of quantized states would allow future quantum computers to be interconnected using the properties of individualized photons or other devices, and this led to Hal's conclusion that if consciousness was just a state, then why not teleport it out of the mind of the dying on some photons into a collective "Brain" with a capital "B." That rhymes with "C," and that stands for "consciousness."

Hal went to MMSC's computers and read everything about Paolo Villoresi and his colleagues at the University of Padova in Italy and a group of scientists from Austria led by Anton Zeilinger. These were the first scientists to develop quantum communications by exchanging single photons from a Japanese low-orbiting satellite to Earth. These guys also identified the exact techniques needed to detect the very weak quantum signal to be exploited in a dedicated satellite. Hal was getting very hopeful as teleportation of the conscious state of a dying human only had to be moved across a room, not from a satellite in space to an Earth station.

We should not be oversimplifying the process. The microscopic structure of the human brain is almost incomprehensibly complicated. It consists of trillions of interconnections among billions of neurons. Exploring the brain's microcircuitry has been done by lining up tiny electrodes within or near single neurons to probe their electrical activity.

There was also an alternate optical approach that used light, but this required labeling neural cells with electrically sensitive dyes that were sometimes toxic to the neurons.

A real advance was the surface plasmon polariton resonance technique. This technique imbeds gold nanoparticles into tissue culture and measures electrical activity of live neurons. This technique takes advantage of a phenomenon known as surface plasmon polarton resonance, which is a sharp spectroscopic resonance at visible/near-infrared wavelengths. The gold nanoparticles are used to optically sense the local electric fields produced when nearby neurons fire. The neuronal activity modulates the electron density at the surface of the nanoparticle, which causes an observable spectral shift that the researcher can monitor—the color. And this, of course, is now all just child's play.

ARE YOU JUST A COMPUTER?

WHAT HAD BEEN SUSPECTED BY DR. Hal Dabble and the scientific community of MMSC for a long time, and also in the underground part of the world of science, was that perhaps our brains were just the organic parts of a pentimate configuration (you remember the Pentium chip) of a computer program. So maybe the answer to consciousness was encoded in the physical structure of the brain itself.

A lot of folks used to think that computers were faster, more powerful, and more capable when compared with the human brain simply because they perform calculations thousands of times faster. Quantitatively measuring the processing power of the human brain has always been a perplexing problem.

One way to attempt this is to measure nerve volume in

the brain and relate it proportionally to processing power. Hal was not too sure that this theory was true, but if it was, it could shortcut the process to a correct estimate of the human brain's processing power.

A great example of all this is the "eyes have it." For a long time scientists understood the neural assemblies of the retina. Medical doctors have been studying the eye for about as far back in time as we can see. What we know structurally and functionally about the eye gives us a window into the human brain's capacity.

The retina is a nerve tissue in the back of the eyeball that detects light and sends images to the brain. A human retina is about a centimeter square, or 0.3997000787 inches square, and is half a millimeter thick. It is made up of 100 million neurons. That's right, 100 million neurons. In order to see, the retina sends light intensity differences to the brain, aimed at particular patches. These images are transported via the optic nerve, which is a million-fiber cable that reaches back into the brain. The retina may process about ten million-point images per second.

The brain is 1,500 cubic centimeters or 100,000 times larger than the retina. By multiplying, we can estimate the processing power of an average brain to be about 100 million MIPS. (MIPS is a million computer instructions per second.)

Just in case you have forgotten your sixth-grade science about how much speed that is, let me remind you with an example. In 1999, the fastest PC processor chip available was a 700 MHz Pentium, which did over 4,200 MIPS. You can see that we would need at least 24,000 processors in a system, or laptop, to match the total speed of the brain. So you could say that our brain is like a 168,000 MHz Pentium computer.

To put this into perspective, remember that back in the twentieth century, people still drove carbon-powered personal transportation devices on the ground. To generate movement, rotation power was applied to wheels that were covered with an organic compound produced from hardened tree sap and reinforced with cords.

The major downfall of these devices was that they emitted exhaust containing compounds and elements that almost terminated the life on the planet until they were replaced by a device that used hydrogen as a fuel, and its exhaust was just water. Anyway, if you used one of these devices, you had to get a permit from some agency of the government to legally operate it on a public road.

As part of the permit process, you were asked if—in the event that you died in an accident operating the device, and hundreds of thousands of people worldwide died each year doing just that—you would donate your body's organs to other people who might need them. For example, they were after eyes, livers, lungs, kidneys, and tissues that could be used by other people. However, the brain was not included on the list. No one ever thought that the brain could be transplanted.

After all the researching, dissecting, and probing of the

brain, still no one had a clue as to what to do with it. The ancient Egyptians, who were good at drying things out so they could be saved, ran a hook up the dead person's nose, removed the brain, and tossed it away. They thought the brain's only function was to produce mucus—to lubricate the body, I guess. They did, however, save the other body organs in jars, I suppose for reinstallation into the body upon reincarnation.

To show you the state of mind in the twentieth century, some people wouldn't hear of giving away their organs when they died. Instead, these folks instructed their survivors to have their corpse drained of its blood, filled with fluid, put in a cement box, and buried in the ground with a marker placed above it on Earth's surface so that dogs could piss on it. Family members could come by and place flowers there, in remembrance for maybe ten years.

This was all rather short-lived, as custom stem cell body parts took over because their installation in your body didn't require you to take drugs. Therefore, the body wouldn't reject the transplanted parts as foreign tissue.

As the use of silicon was exhausted, something had to be found that had greater capacity, and it would be nice if it didn't generate heat above 98.6 °F/ 37 °C. It seemed to be all coming together.

People were finally over the eternity survival panic, the fear of death. That fear had controlled the world and led to all the religions. That fear also birthed the "save the body movements," plastic surgery, replace body parts forever (RBPF), the harvest organ parts movement (HOPM), cryogenics, cloning, custom stem cell grown body parts, and dying in the "passing-on palaces" movements.

Just like in a computer Pentimate configuration reduces us to 0 & 1, On & Off, or Yes & No, and that was something that science can deal with.

WILL THIS MAKE MY HEAD HURT?

WITH MANUFACTURED INTELLIGENCE, THE INTERNATIONAL IN Vitro Meat Association making lab meat, and the medical profession backing off of ethically driven causes, work could proceed without too much government or lunatic interference. So off Hal went to experiment on the edge of knowledge about programming the brain.

The first thing the Montana Mountain Scientific Corporation team did was get some brain tissue to work with. Hal gathered a team around him who knew a lot about stem cell-generated tissue. You can take the seed stem cells (so to speak) and produce brain cells. It had been done before when some people who had had brain injuries or afflictions had their cranium injected with their own stem cells, which then grew to replace the brain's missing or afflicted tissue.

To say the least, there were a few unanswered questions about the tissue. Would the virgin tissue be like a blank slate, a clean blackboard? It should be, because it had never been a brain cell before, and it was not connected to anything that would program it until it grew, got chummy, and fired up.

How would the new tissue be kept viable? Once it grew, how much tissue would be needed? The brain multitasks with one of the systems known as the autonomic nervous system. The brain takes care of things like reminding the heart to beat, the lungs to expand and contract, and the stomach to release chemicals and generally overseeing the body's functions and activity.

But used as a computer, this tissue would not have a body to oversee. All it had to do was think, reason, calculate, and remember everything that was programmed into it. That's all.

Never exposing the new tissue to mundane labors, like overseeing the functioning of a body, allowed the tissue to concentrate on the only stimuli it was going to get: thinking, calculating, and remembering.

The brain solves a problem as if it is searching for a template. The brain literally searches its memory for a stored pattern in the cortex that is analogous to the pattern that would solve the problem or situation you are currently working on. You could describe education as putting patterns in your memory or teaching the neurons to form patterns from experiences on their own. The neat part about this process is the speed. Things happen millisecond by millisecond. But the processing is conducted at different levels of detail, and the wonderful part is that most of this is subliminal. Actually, most of the time you have no idea this is going on. It just happens, and *pow*, the answer pops into your consciousness.

Back in the twentieth century, it took about 24,000 standard laptop computers to even approach the normal brain capacity to just do calculations and monitor body functions, much less think. The potential of the new tissue was huge. But just how physically huge did it need to be? Would it be the size of a bread box or the size of a house? The average brain weighs 3.5 pounds, or 1.36 kilograms. Unlike a computer, which has an on/off switch, the brain has no off switch and is always on in spite of what you think about your brother-in-law.

Would the tissue be able to think about itself and simply grow more of itself if it was placed in the correct nourishing environment of cerebrospinal fluid? That was the hope. If you could start up the tissue and provide it with nourishment, it may just look after itself and grow to the size it needed to be to handle the data.

The idea was that the tissue would "want" to do what it was designed to do. This tissue should have a brain's predisposition, without distorting the data or approaching it with any kind of bias. Programming the start-up was a matter of interfacing the information with the blank tissue via something chemically, or electrically, or more likely a combination of both.

THIS MAKES MY HEAD HURT

SO TO GET THIS ALL STARTED without getting arrested, Hal and the team produced some animal brain tissue. After all, the difference between human genetic codes and the codes of a chimp—or for that matter, a rat—was minimal. At this point, all Hal was looking for was approachable organic tissue instead of silicon to store data on and learn to communicate with it.

The most obvious issue was how to approach the new brain tissue. How was he going to encode it? In creatures (man included), the sensors of the body (seeing, hearing, smelling, and feeling) provided that access. The eyes, ears, nose, and nerve endings gathered the information and then sent it on to the brain for examination, action, and storage.

Brain feedback was the other issue. Creatures could react in all the normal ways. Talking, barking, or chirping were the most obvious signs that the brain wanted to be heard. The autonomic nervous system gave positive feedback, most of it on a subliminal level, to feelings or nerve stimulation by responding to stimulus with muscle reaction. Put your hand in a fire and watch the muscles react by with drawing the hand. Or when a man sees a good-looking girl, he gets an erection. You know the drill. So now what was to be done?

First, the team at MMSC dragged out all of the medical devices that were electric or mechanical in nature. These were all of the devices that had been invented by medical professionals to help injured or afflicted people who had lost limb, sensing devices, or organs. They first removed the mechanical part of the device and then upgraded the software and electrical components.

It was a good place to start, and by altering these devices and growing stem cell nerve tissue to connect them with the brain tissue, meaningful communication was getting under way.

The group of scientists who had accomplished this were beginning to get noticed. Awards were being presented, and people were being named as the science men and women of the year. Once you are noticed, you can either go public or you can go underground. Hal felt the underground route seemed to be best, so he stayed put in his Montana science center and just avoided satellite teleconferencing and any form of communication with what was left of the news media.

Encoded photons via stem cell nerve pathways seemed to be the route to take. The question now became what should be put into the virgin brain tissue and to what use. This was where the cult of the passing-on palaces surfaced again.

The people who ran the passing-on palaces asked for a meeting and arrived with a box of encoded silicon chips and a box of money. They made a very convincing argument to Hal's scientific management committee at MMSC that the information they had been trusted with was the perfect raw material, as it was the last will and testament of folks who had been waiting to get into some living tissue again. On top of that, it was perfectly legal. They had all signed every kind of legal release the best lawyers in the known world could have thought up at that time.

The other extremely attractive aspect of this argument was the box of money. Along with signed releases, the folks whose consciousness now resided, it was hoped, on these silicon chips had funded the passing-on palaces cult generously. So the holders of the chips had all the chips they needed to play the game, no matter what the table stakes were.

To quote a twentieth-century TV game show, everybody involved said, "Let's make a deal." And so they did. The passing-on palaces people would agree to fund the remaining research for what they hoped would be the completion of encoding brain tissue with the digital material with which they had been entrusted. Once this information was alive again, the cult officers and managers could take the fund's remaining money and run. If it didn't work, it didn't matter to them, because they had fulfilled their contracts. If it worked and people liked the idea, once the general population got wind of its success, the company could gear up again and take over the world where religions had left off. It was a win-win situation.

A CRAP SHOOT

A LOT OF PEOPLE IN THE science industry would like you to think that science is very serious business. You must have heard the old twentieth-century expression regarding the simplicity of something: "It's not rocket science." This means, of course, that rocket science—and by inference, any scientific undertaking—is serious.

Just how serious the selection process in science had become is best illustrated by the process used by Hal's MMSC team in choosing which silicon chips were to be used for encoding the blank brain tissue. A lot of corporate time was spent speculating about what earth-shattering knowledge or mind should or would contribute the first information and/or consciousness to be implanted in the virgin brain tissue.

How could scientists select the initial data to launch what may become the most revolutionary and important leap in the history of mankind? So they came up with a clever random selection process.

First, the chips were inert. They did not require much care and were reasonably impervious to normal heat, cold, and shock. Unlike frozen bodies, where an increase in temperature could produce some rather foul results, the chips were put into trays and stored in, for lack of a better description, cardboard boxes about the size of a ream of paper. And like a standard case of ten reams of paper, there were ten ream-size boxes in each case. The passing-on palace's people had randomly selected twelve cases of chips that they had brought with them. The scientists randomly drew a number from one to twelve and selected box seven.

The box was opened, and the chips were removed from the trays and placed with care—okay, they were dumped—into a soft-sided box. Now the selection!

A couple of the MMSC scientists located a seven-year-old child playing in the child-care area in one of the offices of the scientific management offices. He was the son of one of the scientists who got stuck with babysitting duty that day, as his wife was in law class. They told the kid to cover his eyes, put his hand in the box, and draw out a chip. He did, and they all cheered. The first chip had been selected. Now that's serious science.

MEN ARE NOT FROM MARS

DO YOU SUPPOSE THERE IS GOING to be a gender issue with the BB? Hal thought. For some reason, it just had not occurred to the scientists that once the chips were downloaded into the BB, there could be a gender issue. Back in 1992, John Gray wrote a book called *Men Are from Mars, Women Are from Venus.* Essentially, it was about the difference in the way men and women were believed to think. It had nothing to do with the origin of the species or space exploration.

It was simply a metaphor, but now that the solar system has been somewhat explored and selectively colonized, everyone knows that men did not come from Mars (although some men are camped out there now) and women did not come from Venus. The metaphor seemed to accidentally hold up, though. The surface of Mars is solid, cold, hard, reasonably unforgiving, and requires vigilance to exist on it. On the other hand, Venus appears ethereal, gaseous, with no solid ground, and whirls around at great speed with no apparent value or reason but to keep itself together in a very large gaseous sphere.

Now there are some people who could take the previous paragraph the wrong way, but back in the late 1900s and early 2000s, there certainly were gender differences. It is hard to believe now what they were based on—of all things, sex! That's right, sex.

One of the major scientific advances of all times in liberating women and in removing gender competition and inequality was the discovery that women didn't even need men's sperm to have a baby. In the early 2000s, it was learned that by gene manipulation, a woman could have a baby without a man at all. This was, of course, a massive blow to men's egos and had far-flung effects on almost everything for a while.

Imagine. If women didn't need men to have a baby, what did they need them for? From the dawn of time, sex and the drive to procreate had been the driving force after the survival force. The entire changing sequence started off with reliable chemical birth control, which in the mid-1900s freed women up to have intercourse without the fear of having a pregnancy.

There really were some ridiculous carryings-on over this entire issue, and silicon, not the chip type, played a role in some of it. Apparently, women and men in those days spent an inordinate amount of time trying to attract each other.

Many people worldwide adapted a Stone Age practice of decorating their bodies with colored pigments placed under the skin with needles, making designs that they believed, when they were naked, would make them extra attractive to the opposite sex. People also participated in an African tribal practice of piercing areas of their body with studs and gems. Few places on the body were immune to this procedure, so you could find studs sticking out of an ear, tongue, or, God forbid, a male's foreskin.

But back to silicon. In the dance of the sexes for attention, women had been trained to obsess over their breast size and shape. These glands, which were simply to provide milk for an offspring, had become an object of a major industry. To illustrate how silly it all was, imagine going to a medical doctor and having him cut a slit under the breasts and implant pouches of liquid silicon or, later, pouches of salt water in the breasts so that they stood out from the body and were larger so that they could be more easily noticed by men.

To illustrate how ridiculous things became, women with naturally large breasts went to medical doctors and had them surgically reduced. Women typically said that their clothing would fit better after their breast size was adjusted.

Clothing, of course, was now designed to expose as much of the breast as possible. But for some reason exposing the nipple on the breast was not acceptable, so clothing was developed to push the breast up and out, making it look large and inviting, but not exposing the nipple. The breast packaging and presentation industry became a billion-dollar-a-year business. If you want more on this, locate the book *Uplift*, the story of the women's undergarment industry. Imagine a culture obsessed with this kind of foolishness.

Men, however, were just as nuts. Male penis size was the holy grail of male pride. When a man's penis function began to fail as he aged or got less interested in sex, he would take pills to get blood to flow to the penis so it would be erect. Some men were so overwhelmed with the fear of loss of this function that they had pumps implanted in their penis so they could "get it up."

So man went from jumping any lady that he could in the cave to keep the race going, to taking eggs from a woman's body, fertilizing them in a petri dish, and putting them back into the woman so she could grow the baby and then deliver it at term.

With man's sperm now being taken out of the process and people happy with themselves the way they are, gender competition has become a thing of the past. However, some of the chips that would be downloaded from the passing-on palace's vaults could be old enough to start all of the preceding nonsense again, at least in the brain, which apparently is the seat of all the crazy sex-drive problems anyway.

KEEP ME IN THE LOOP

THE MEETINGS AT MMSC WERE NOW all about connecting tissue, not the kind of tissue that holds your body together and wraps your organs to keep everything in its place. Stem cells fabricated the kind of tissue that would hopefully take the downloaded digital electrical information stored on the chip and teleport it to the brain's tissue so that the vacant brain had something to think about. Control of single photon teleportation in the brain gave science an indisputable and incorruptible vehicle attributed historically only to godlike creatures.

Would the brain then look at itself, and what would it do? The theory was that it would organize whatever was presented. However, because it was ignorant, how would it know how to organize? It was common knowledge that the brain had to be educated so it would have analogous patterns to use as the template for problem solving. However, perhaps the folks from the passing-on palaces didn't want the chips to be used to solve problems. They were the problems.

All the chip information wanted was to be recognized as valuable, paid attention to for its knowledge and accomplishments, asked its opinion about things, and be respected. Boy, doesn't that sound familiar!

The crux was the same thing that existed right after man developed far enough so that survival was reasonably assured. If your belly was full, you had shelter, species reproduction was available, and there was a good chance that you would make it through the night to the next day, recognition, respect, and authority raised their ugly head.

Once you put the chip's information into a memory device, the BB should realize that it didn't need to be fed, and it had no control of and did not care about its shelter. The only real concerns were how it made its opinions known, how it expressed itself, and how it got the respect it wanted. Because of all the efforts MMSC had demonstrated to provide the BB with the proper environment, the brain would just take for granted the sufficient surroundings and thrive.

This seems to have a very familiar ring.

REMEMBER ME?

TELEPORTING, CHEMICALLY ENCODING, ELECTRICAL RESONANT defining, photon simulation, imbedding nanoparticles, and plasmon polariton resonance: this is just a partial list of ideas and techniques that were addressed as communication with the new tissue in the BB was attempted.

The tissue was inert. It just sort of sat there and didn't do much. It did stay alive and seemed to adjust to the comfortable, nutritive environment provided by the Montana scientists.

They wanted to get down to the task. Hall wondered how they would accomplish taking this digital information and introducing it to virginal tissue without using the body's sensing devices. The living person, of course, had eyes, ears, and nerves connected to the brain. The process was straightforward. These sensing devices gathered sights, sounds, and tissue impulses, converted them to electrochemical and mechanical signals and, via nerve pathways, got the impulses to the correct part of the cortex that processed the information.

A lot of time was spent looking for a clearinghouse somewhere in the brain that noticed, recorded, or remembered things because the primal impulses were switched to the correct place in the brain. This clearinghouse could be compared to the PBX of the late-nineteenth-century telephone systems.

Then, a telephone operator ran the PBX. A PBX is essentially a large board with holes in it and plugs on telephone cords that were manually connected by the operator when some person wanted to be connected to someone else in order to exchange information. Up until the twenty-first century, people had telephones that were connected by wires to the central PBX. (At this point, it had been refined and was called a switch.)

That may seem hard to believe, but telephones were wired to plugs in the home. The wires from the phones were strung out of the house, into the street, to the poles, and to the phone company's offices. Once the signal on that piece of wire got to the office, the PBX operator connected that phone to any other phone, almost anywhere in the world, and the two people could talk. It was considered very clever, and this system was set up worldwide. I am sure this rings a bell from some history class. In any case, this was well before universal communication nodes (phones) were implanted into infants' heads at two months of age and the infants were assigned a permanent phone number that was engraved (tattooed) on them, near their private parts.

A lot of thought went into the implanted communication nodes, as you can imagine what would happen if you couldn't turn off your phone, put it on hold, or determine what you talked about, who you talked to, when you communicated, and where you communicated. It also took some training to become adept at using this device. The device had no physical switches. It was all controlled by your brain waves. Back in the twentieth century, the only thing somewhat comparable was the annoyingly common and irritating practice of texting on cell phones. This procedure was primarily a juvenile exercise and a waste of time. It did accomplish some good, though, by exercising the thumbs, as keys on these primitive cell phones were extremely small.

After spending an inordinate amount of time and effort looking for the brain's switch, it was discovered that there wasn't one. The brain's electrical system flooded the brain with chemical messengers, and the correct area of the brain simply used the right chemical message to transmit the data to the proper area.

This "flooding" was not really a flood. The brain's moist transmission fluid could hardly be called a flood. It was the mere suggestion of a nuance of an infinitesimally small change in some chemical molecular potential that took the message, routed it to the proper place, and waited for another molecular change so that it could get back to the other cells with the answer. If I said that this all took place in the blink of an eye, it would be like saying that all politicians were saints.

The speed at which this all took place was mind-boggling. But if the brain chemicals did their job, then the speed of the transmission and the search for the correct location for the message to be delivered was a foregone conclusion and would be handled automatically. And it was.

Hal always thought that it would boil down to chemistry and was elated with the team's new findings.

In one of the endless meetings, one very sarcastic and frustrated scientist said that he was sick and tired of being the mother to this glob of tissue. It's funny where good ideas come from. That is exactly what the BB needed, a mother.

Mothers teach the kids (in this case, the brain) from the ground up. But how? Well, they just repeat themselves, and the kids learns through repetition.

FROM PBX TO NEUROTHEOLOGY

YES, NEUROTHEOLOGY, NOT TO BE CONFUSED with that used by
Aldous Huxley in his utopian novel *Island*. Neurotheology is
the study of the cognitive neuroscience of religious experience
and spirituality. This was one of the last-ditch efforts to
support religions during their last profitable years.

In what seemed to be an endless discussion with the MMSC
team, Hal said that the basic idea is that we are hardwired to
believe in a God. Huxley used this concept in its philosophical
context as he tried to explain all of the madness of the world.
Put another way, neurotheology, which has also been called
biotheology or spiritual neuroscience, is the study of neural
phenomena with subjective experiences of spirituality and
hypotheses to explain these phenomena. In the 1960s there

was a lot of this, but they were called drug trips and could land you in jail.

The same old thing was being looked for: self-awareness and consciousness, which made everyone unique. More specifically, one of the theories stated that a preformal development in humans created an illusion of chronological time as a fundamental part of normal adult cognition past the age of three. This next idea is that this inability of adults to retrieve earlier experienced images from infancy creates questions, such as "Where did I come from?" and the old favorite, "Where does it all go?" This suggests the creation of various religious explanations. The death experience as a peaceful regression into timelessness as the brain dies (a nice way to put it) was one more attempt to keep the collection plates full and nontaxable real estate off the property tax rolls.

The practitioners of this cult used the main twentieth-century religious tools by performing repetitive, rhythmic stimulation. Remember the Roman mass with music? Or how about dancing naked around a fire in the jungle? Human rituals with rhythmic stimulation contribute to the delivery of transcendental feelings of connection to a universal unit. Those feelings were also obtainable with the use of street drugs, so the "priests" of this idea said that physical stimulation alone was not sufficient to generate transcendental unitive experiences. For that to occur, there must be a blending of the rhythmic stimulation with ideas. If that can occur, then rituals turn a meaningful idea into a visceral experience.

They preached that folks are compelled to act out myths by the biological operations of the brain on account of what they called the "inbuilt tendency of the brain to turn thoughts into action." That thought bothered Hal. What the hell would they do if the BB had these properties transplanted into it along with the states of consciousness from the digital silicon chips? Worse yet, what if the damn thing wanted to turn thoughts into action?

If you really want to research this, read *Modern Neurology* and *The Question of God* by Eugen Drewermann. These were published back in 2006 and 2007 and are out of print, but I am sure they can be found in some computer somewhere. These books dealt seriously with the then-radical ideas of traditional conceptions of a God and the soul via a sweeping reinterpretation of religion in the light of neurology.

It was also said that an increase in N, N-dimethyltryptamine levels in the pineal gland formed the basis of a spiritual experience that simply arose from this increase. It was given credit for the perception that time, fear, or self-consciousness had dissolved. It was to give you oneness with the universe, spiritual awe, ecstatic trances, sudden enlightenment, and, best of all, an altered state of consciousness. These claims were disputed by the street drug dealers of the day, and they put the neurotheologists on their hit lists.

Other methodology in the mid-1900s attempted to use

EEGs to study brain wave patterns, correlating them with "spiritual" states. By stimulating the temporal lobes of human subjects (students) by using weak magnetic fields and then stronger magnetic fields, scientists claimed they could induce sensations of "an ethereal presence in the room." Some students will say anything to get good grades, and it was never resolved as to the mechanism that may have elicited the response.

Studies using neuroimaging a few years later tried to localize brain region activity during experiences that the subjects associated with "spiritual" feelings or images. It was decided that there was a common core among people that was a reflection of structures of spiritual experience across cultures, history, and religions. Feelings associated with religious experience are normal aspects of brain function under extreme circumstances, rather than communication from God. Those conclusions didn't seem to satisfy anyone.

PLEASE LISTEN

"HOW DO WE COMMUNICATE WITH A BB?" That was the only heading on the meeting's agenda that morning. It was Hal's and the entire MMSC team's major concern. After all, the big brain has no visual cortex, no audio inputs, and can't feel a thing. Each of these stimuli had one thing in common. Whatever was being learned was converted to chemical electrical impulses.

At first, the team took stem cell-generated optic nerve tissue, made an optic nerve cable, and connected one end to an electronic TV camera (for lack of a better term) and the other end to the tissue. They then played visual material, which did stimulate the BB, but with no frame of reference, the scientists could see it would take too long to teach the brain anything of consequence. Someone had forgotten that Mom had a lifetime to teach Sonny. The scientists didn't think they did.

The chips contained sophisticated material, not just unfocused colors and shapes. At least that's what science thought.

The same kind of drill was tried with audio. In people sounds are sensed by the auditory nerve system. These sounds are converted from vibrations into electrical signals that the brain compares to other electrical signals and so people hear. However, this new brain didn't have to hear. It just took the signals and dealt directly with them. It had already eliminated the ears, eardrums, cilia, and all the mechanical devices in the human auditory system that converted the sound into intelligible electrical impulses that the brain could deal with.

However, hearing really wasn't required by the chip's information. It had no relationship with the Les and Larry Elgart album, *Best of the Big Bands, Vol. 1* (a lot more on that later). On the chip was the electronic chemical impressions, a feeling that had been created by the old brain when it interpreted the music and generated emotional values, which had been converted to digital material and now wanted to get out and be experienced again.

These impulses then made everything happen. So why not just put the digital information electrically into the brain and watch what would happen? So they did.

A BIG MISTAKE WAS ABOUT TO HAPPEN

HAL WAS LOSING A LOT OF sleep and was very concerned, as some rather alarming questions still remained. What if the first random chip that was put into the BB was from someone who, although accomplished and brilliant, was needy? What if, after a lifetime of education, accomplishments, wealth, fame, and recognition, that person was empty? To the outside world, there could not be much more the person could give, get, accomplish, or conduct.

No one knows what is in a person's private place. No one!

Hidden in a person's consciousness is the only private material or place they can have. The great lovers of the world have always tried to explain what they were and what they felt.

For the first six months of a relationship, when everything is growing, glowing, and going well, the most precious hope of lovers is that at last they have found someone to take the time to absorb their internal feelings that, up to that time, have been kept a total secret.

Then it always happens. Both lovers get lost in themselves. Who would think that the most important item in the intimate internal parts of Albert Einstein (E = mc2) never revealed to anyone were the feelings that were liberated by a song?

Who in his right mind could conceive that Les and Larry Elgart's version of "Skyliner" in *Best of the Big Bands Vol. 1* was perhaps the catalyst that produced E = mc2. "Skyliner" was a song about an airplane with four engines, not even the supersonic Concord, a plane that was hurrying home to the one you loved. "Skyliner: was recorded by the Elgart brothers when there were four tracks on the recording studio's control consuls.

With that kind of simple and straightforward recording equipment, all the musicians had to play the music perfectly, at least once, all at the same time. It made the musicians do it right. All of them. Did it right. At the same time.

This album came out in the first half of the twentieth century, before dubbing, thirty-two channels, and digital hard-drive recorders. To get the sound they wanted—a live, clear, clean, precise, crisp version—the Elgart brothers went down to the local Hollywood lumberyard and bought four-by-eight-feet sheets of plywood. They then bought varnish and brushes, sealed the plywood sheets with varnish, and gave them a second and third coat. They took these panels to the recording studio and set them up behind the horn sections of the orchestra. This hard surface acted as a mirror and reflected the horn's sounds with a clarity and life never heard before in recorded music.

This sound was exactly the result they were after, a live, exquisite, vibrant sound that simply came alive out of the vacuum tube hi-fi systems of that era with a live quality that was infectious.

Perhaps somewhere on what's left of the Internet is a website where you can look up "Elgart, Les, and Larry." Then search for "Best of the Big Bands, Vol. 1," and if you're lucky, punch up the song "Skyliner." The new BB was stuck with a million situations like this.

Hal and the science team were beginning to realize that what was turning out to be important to the consciousnesses, which had been captured, recorded, digitalized, and saved on silicon, was important to the individual who had never expressed in life that which no one else cared about or only gave cursory value to.

Emotionally generated values, exclusive to whomever, were the key to the consciousness and self-awareness that had been saved on the chips.

No one ever could have seen that coming. Hal and everyone thought great wisdom, thoughts, values, creative understanding, experiences, and a vast storehouse of incredible insight would be released when the chips were decoded. No one thought it would be chops or a melody that Einstein wanted to replay and be remembered.

The lesson being learned was the absolute absurdity of life. The certainness of oblivion. The total inability of future generations to be able to take advantage of the past as a template for tomorrow.

This information was so controversial and upsetting that it was put into the same category as life existing elsewhere in the universe. Of course, rumors circulated, but the powers that made decisions for the masses followed the same successful template that had kept the knowledge of extraterrestrial life a secret from the public for hundreds of years.

Because there was no longer a God, what was becoming painfully clear was the simple fact that we are all special and unique individuals. Maybe even God. We all create ourselves. Isn't that what a God is supposed to do?

Because we are born with a virgin brain, unprogrammed and empty, we must all start at the same place. What was becoming so apparent was that differences may arise simply because of tissue ability and chemical imbalances.

How very simple. How completely complex.

POSTSCRIPT

WHAT COULD IT BE ABOUT THE Les and Larry Elgart rendition of "Skyliner" that Albert Einstein's brain wanted to save? Einstein had been made an icon of the ages and was declared the most forward and imaginative thinker ever born. Yet, when Einstein's self-awareness was decoded, no one seemed to understand the emotional impact of a melody. It was almost unthinkable that Einstein's legacy to the ages, and the only clue left as a gift to science by this man's incredible mind, baffled everyone, except Hal.

Having done all the work he could think of on this master of mysteries, Hal finally sat down, had a few glasses of wine (a good California zinfandel), and connected himself to what had replaced headphones. By this point in time, everyone was hardwired at birth so audio inputs came with the body as well as video accessibility and your own control number, which of course kept you in touch.

Hal simply called up the Elgart melody, turned off the lights, sat in the dark, and listened. What could be the idea behind this pleasant melody that may have changed the world, unleashed untold energy, and produced an equation that launched a future for the world that was still unfolding?

Hal simply couldn't find a thing, so he fed the melody into the universal computer banks, the sort of Google of the future. He queried this repository of collective knowledge. First he asked what this melody was. The response from the computer was instantaneous: **Skyliner.** (The time it takes the universal computer to respond is represented by dots [……..]. The more dots, the longer it took.) *What did it mean?* **It was a twentieth-century swing band melody, having to do with air transportation, with a rhythm designed for dancing.** *What is meant by dancing?* ... **Moving the body to express oneness with the melody.** *Why was this important?* ….. **Oneness is one of the goals of man and the rhythm of life.** *Who thought that life was about moving to a rhythm? .* **Unknown.** *What is a melody made of? ..* **Notes.** *Where are the notes? .* **On a scale.** *What makes notes different? ...* **Time signatures, volume, the way they are expressed, and the complex addition of harmonics.** *How can notes be combined?* ... **Any way you desire.** *Are there rules to accomplish this combination?* ……….. **Not rules, but accepted guidelines generated by social issues.** *What happens if these guidelines are broken? ...* **Nothing. In some cases the breaking of the guidelines produces new structures that are revolutionary**

and pleasing. *Can melodies made of notes be compared to equations? ..* **They can be.** *Is it possible to build or write an equation from a melody? ……..* **It is possible.** *What would these equations look like? ……….* **It would depend upon the template and results equated.** *Are the underlying templates of music equations? ……* **Yes, but most are primitive.** *Are the notes, then, numbers or values? ….* **Yes, they can be, but it is more complicated than that.** *Where do melodies and equations come from? ……….* **Unknown.** *Could melodies be equations that we do not understood? ……* **Yes.** *Can you write an equation from a melody? ……..* **Yes.** *Would I be able to understand it? ……..* **No, you would perhaps understand the melody but not why it was appealing to you. It is an equation of appeal.** *Am I also an equation? …………* **You are. The internal equation that you are may be sequenced to a melody, and in some cases sequenced equations combine and solve each other and, in doing so, reveal a completely new idea, unknown and foreign.** *How would those ideas be expressed? …………* **In a new equation.** *So is there no end to this? ……* **There is an end.** *Can we, you and I, put together a search for the equation that is Skyliner? …* **I have no template for that search.** *Can we detect possible equations in Skyliner by cross referencing the Einstein E = mc2 equation with all the possible ways to display Skyliner as an equation? …………………………………………………………………………* **Fascinating.**

TODAY by Clem Stein

There's Meals on Wheels,
Safe automobiles?
The government steals and then backs the deals,
Small claims court appeals.
Nothing any longer is left to chance,
Your ass is covered in advance
So that you can't lose your pants.
All the risks are covered
So that all the joys are left undiscovered.
The iPod and MP3 nonsense
Is only outdone by cell phone conversations' contents.
With no longer a need to navigate,
A map need no longer articulate.
You know where you are all the time
But have no concept of kind.
With love on everyone's lips
And excessive food on everyone's hips,
You accelerate down the road
While texting nonsense like a toad.
Your life is a moment of now,
With not one thought of when or how.
You just do it all, right now
For reasons that were programmed in you somehow.
With words like wait, fate, discipline, and hate no longer there
Life is as empty as an unseated chair.
With systems in place to cover your bottom

There never seems to be a problem,
So you go out and celebrate
And never expect the next Watergate.
Then, when you're hit from behind
All you're able to do is whine.
There you sit in a sports bar,
Drinking your Bud Light out of a jar,
Screaming at the big screen,
"We're number one."
God, don't you sound dumb,
Rewarding hand/eye coordination
As if it were an orgasmic sensation.
All it is, is a developed accident,
Which sometimes bypasses the brain's intent.
Sports keeps us all from thinking about ourselves,
As watching the games puts us up on shelves.
But of course you're a sport
Looking for thrills,
But perhaps lacking some of the skills,
So you take one of those pills.
Now a four-hour erection is one of the ills.
What to do? Not a problem.
Search the net
And it may stop throbbing.
Of course it's never your fault.
Entitlement is what it's all about.
The old saw about parental wisdom
Has been put aside as a schism.
So you go off to the gym,
Jumping up and in,

Sweating out your designer water.
All you are is advertising's fodder.
You have become such a fool
And just continue to drool Starbucks's gruel.
If they close six hundred stores
And they lock up all the doors,
Perhaps we can have new wars.
They're fun, they're great, and they're a cure?